The Railway Kitten

The Railway Kitten

Holly Webb
Illustrated by Sophy Williams

LITTLE TIGER
LONDON

This book was inspired by Fanny, the Gipsy Hill Station Cat

LITTLE TIGER
An imprint of Little Tiger Press Limited
1 Coda Studios, 189 Munster Road, London SW6 6AW

Imported into the EEA by Penguin Random House Ireland,
Morrison Chambers, 32 Nassau Street, Dublin D02 YH68

www.littletiger.co.uk

A paperback original
First published in Great Britain in 2023

Text copyright © Holly Webb, 2023
Illustrations copyright © Sophy Williams, 2023
Author photograph © Charlotte Knee Photography

ISBN: 978-1-78895-565-2

A CIP catalogue record for this book is available from the British Library.

Printed and bound in the UK.

MIX
Paper | Supporting
responsible forestry
FSC® C171272

The Forest Stewardship Council® (FSC®) is a global, not-for-profit
organization dedicated to the promotion of responsible forest management
worldwide. FSC defines standards based on agreed principles for
responsible forest stewardship that are supported by environmental, social,
and economic stakeholders. To learn more, visit www.fsc.org

10 9 8 7 6 5 4 3 2 1

Chapter One

"Don't forget your lunch!" Mum called out and Scarlett darted back into the kitchen with a squeak – she nearly had.

Mum was doing up the straps of Poppy's pushchair, ready for the dash down the road to the station. They were lucky that it was nearby – close enough for the sound of trains to help Scarlett drift off to sleep at night and wake her up every morning. Still, they always seemed to be in a rush to make it in time for the train to school.

Scarlett dragged her coat on and they hurried along the road – with Poppy still eating her banana from breakfast.

"That was close – oh, the train's late," Mum said, looking up at the screen as they passed the ticket office. "Poor Poppy, I could have let you finish that banana at home. Oh, sweetheart, you've got it all down your front." She pulled out some wipes from her bag and started trying to clean Poppy up while Scarlett slumped sleepily on to one of the benches on the platform.

She was peering down the railway tracks, looking for the train, when something soft nudged her leg, just

above her sock. Scarlett jumped, for
a horrible moment thinking it was a
spider – she really didn't like spiders.
But when she looked down, there was
a small, dark, furry face staring back
at her. A kitten! A tiny black-and-
orange kitten.

"Hey…" Scarlett whispered. "What are you doing under there?"

The kitten mewed – a squeaky, demanding noise as if it wanted something. Then it ducked back further underneath the bench, looking startled, and Scarlett realized the train was coming.

"Oh, I wish we didn't have to go," Scarlett whispered as she scrambled up from the bench and headed after Mum and Poppy. "Bye, kitten. I really hope I see you again…"

Scarlett kept remembering the kitten all day at school. She'd only had a very quick glimpse of it before the train scared it back into the shadows but she was sure she'd never seen a cat with markings like that before. Its face had been half gingery and half black, a bit like a mask.

When they got back to the station that afternoon, Scarlett looked eagerly across the tracks to the other platform, hoping to see the kitten peeping out from under the bench again. But all she could see were pigeons.

"Are you OK, Scarlett?" Mum called to her. "Did you see someone from school?"

"No, I was looking for the kitten," Scarlett explained. "The one I saw this morning. With the orange-and-black fur."

"Oh, yes. Tortoiseshell, that's what they're called. I wonder where she's come from – she can't live at the station. Let's try and be early tomorrow in case she's around."

Scarlett nodded eagerly. "Please! She's so pretty, Mum. I want you to see her."

When they reached the station the next morning, there were only a few people scattered along the platform as the next train wasn't due for a few minutes. Scarlett hurried over to the bench where she'd seen the kitten the day before, and Mum followed with the pushchair. Poppy was leaning out to look too – Scarlett didn't think her little sister knew what they were looking for but she was definitely excited.

"Oh…" Scarlett sighed sadly. "It's not here."

But Mum laughed. "Look behind you."

Poppy was pointing and bouncing up

and down in the pushchair. "Meow!" she squeaked and Scarlett swung round.

The kitten was gazing out at her from the weeds growing along the edge of the railings. It was half hidden in the plants, its dark, gingery fur melting into the shadows.

"Hello…" Scarlett slowly stretched out one hand and the kitten leaned forwards a little to sniff her fingers and then nudge its chin against them gently. "You're in disguise," she whispered. "That's very clever."

"I love the little gingery striped tail," Mum said. "Is there a name tag on that collar, Scarlett? Does it say what the kitten's called?"

Scarlett rubbed the top of the kitten's head and tried to look at the collar but all she could see was a phone number. "I don't think so... I can't tell if it's a girl or a boy kitten either."

"I think she has to be a girl," Mum said thoughtfully. "Gran's old cat was tortoiseshell. Do you remember Patches? You might not have been old enough. Anyway, I'm sure Gran told me that tortoiseshell cats are almost always girls."

The kitten was getting a bit more confident. She padded out to wind herself around Scarlett's ankles and now they could see her properly. "She's got black whiskers on her dark fur side, and white ones on the ginger side," Scarlett said, laughing. "I didn't even know cats could do that."

"Oh, Scarlett, the train's coming."

"Stay back there," Scarlett told the kitten. She supposed the little cat probably knew that trains were dangerous and she shouldn't get near the edge of the platform, but she was still very little.

They hurried on to the train and Scarlett stood against a window, looking out to check everything was OK. The kitten had tucked herself safely away in the weeds at the edge of the railings again and Scarlett breathed a sigh of relief.

From then on, Mum and Poppy and Scarlett looked out for the kitten every day. Other passengers at the station made a fuss of her too but Scarlett was sure that the kitten loved them best. She always came padding along the platform to say hello and she'd lost a lot of her shyness.

"She likes you, doesn't she?" one of the station staff said, a couple of weeks later. Tony, it said on his name badge.

"I think so," Scarlett agreed shyly. "Do you know who she belongs to? Does she live at the station?"

Tony reached down to tickle the kitten under her chin. "I don't know, to be honest. She just turned up a while ago. She doesn't sleep here though. I think she lives in one of the houses just down the road, I've seen her heading into the gardens along there."

He grinned at Scarlett and pulled something out of his pocket – a crinkly foil packet. "Don't tell anyone…" he whispered, scattering a few cat treats in front of the kitten, who snaffled them eagerly. "I shouldn't feed someone else's cat but she always looks so hungry."

"I was worried she was a bit thin!" Scarlett agreed.

"Here." Tony held out the packet and dropped a couple of the little crunchy treats into Scarlett's hand. "You have a go. She loves them."

Scarlett crouched down and held out the treats, and the kitten nuzzled into her hand to gobble them up. It was the best feeling, that velvety little chin tickling against her palm. Scarlett couldn't help laughing.

The kitten's ears pricked up as she felt the rumbling along the tracks that meant another train was coming. She'd seen so many of them now, she wasn't scared any more. But she still liked to make sure she was tucked well out of the way. Some of the trains didn't stop, swooshing straight through the station in a wild rush of air that ruffled her fur and threatened to lift her off her paws. Even the trains that did stop were noisy and then crowds of people would pour out on to the platform, not always watching where they were putting their feet.

The kitten skittered away to hide under a bench, watching as the train pulled in to the platform across the tracks. She was almost sure that this was the train the girl came back on. It was always about the same time and she'd seen the girl's mum and little sister in the pushchair not that long before.

She would see them when the train pulled out of the platform and then a few minutes later they'd come out of the

doors that opened by the stairs. The girl
would stroke her and fuss over her and
maybe even give her a little something
to eat. The kitten was hungry and no one
was at home to let her in and feed her.
Her owners put her out in the morning
and usually didn't come home till late –
she was always starving by then.

Passengers were starting to hurry
down the stairs now and the kitten crept
along the side of the ticket office, where
she had a good view of the lift. The doors
slid open and there they were. They
were looking for her too, she could tell.
The kitten darted along the platform,
mewing eagerly, and rubbed against the
girl's ankles.

Her loud, rumbling purrs sounded just
like a train.

Chapter Two

"Look, there's a seat over there,
Abbie."

Scarlett looked up and saw the new
girl from her class coming towards
her. She had only joined the school
last week and looked shy, as if she
wasn't sure if she ought to sit down, so
Scarlett smiled and moved her bag to
make more room.

"Hello! I'm Scarlett. We're in the same maths group?"

Abbie sat down. "Yes! Sorry. I'm still learning everyone's name."

"It must be hard starting school in the middle of the term," Scarlett agreed. "Do you like it so far?"

Abbie nodded. "Yeah… I miss my old school but everyone's been really nice." She nodded towards a woman with a baby in a sling who was sitting near the doors. "That's my mum and my little brother Jonas."

"My mum's over there, with my sister in the pushchair." Scarlett pointed. "She's called Poppy."

"Do you get this train every day?" Abbie asked.

"Mostly. Not Thursdays because I do

judo after school. Which station do you get off at?"

"Parson Road. Our new house is just a bit along from the station."

"Me too!" Scarlett beamed at her. There were a few people from school who caught the train but no one else in her class. It would be great to have someone to talk to on the journey. "We're about five minutes up the road."

It seemed natural to keep on chatting as they got off the train. Scarlett's mum said hello to Abbie's mum and they started talking about the school and where the best toddler group was. Abbie and her mum, whose name was Lara, came down in the lifts with them and then Scarlett nudged her. "Have you seen the station kitten yet?"

Abbie smiled delightedly. "No, is there really a kitten that lives here?"

"I don't think she actually lives in the

station but her home must be close by,"
Scarlett explained. "She's always around
and she likes to come and say hello to
us. Look, over there!" She pointed out
the little tortoiseshell kitten, who was
padding along the platform towards
them, with a cautious look at Abbie and
her mum.

"Oh! I know her!" Abbie said,
crouching down to hold out a hand to
the kitten. "She lives next door to us. It is
the same kitten, isn't it, Mum?"

"I'm pretty sure it is," her mum agreed.
"Her markings are so unusual. There
can't be two kittens like that around
here."

"She's called Whiskers. I asked the
man who owns her," Abbie explained.
Then she looked up at Scarlett

worriedly. "She was sitting on the front wall waiting for him to come home. I don't think they've got a cat flap, so she's outside all the time. Even when it's raining! And then yesterday, she came in through our kitchen window! I think she'd climbed up the fire escape. She ate some of the cheese I was grating for Mum – she was starving."

"Abbie, you mustn't let someone else's cat come into our flat," her mum said – and it sounded like she'd said it a lot. "And you mustn't feed them! She doesn't belong to us *and* the landlord's got a no pets rule!"

"She isn't *our* pet!" Abbie pointed out. "But I know what you mean." She watched their mums heading for the station exit and said to Scarlett, "It just makes me sad seeing her out there. She always looks so hungry."

"She does," Scarlett agreed. "I guess that's why she comes here – because she's lonely and cold." She glanced round the station and added in a whisper, "I've got half a tuna sandwich in my lunchbox."

"Abbie, Scarlett's mum has invited us round for a cup of tea," Abbie's mum called. "Come on."

Scarlett scrabbled around in her bag for her lunchbox and pulled out the sandwich, waving it temptingly at the kitten. "Whiskers, come on. We'll leave it outside for you. We might get in trouble if we feed you here."

The kitten gave an eager little mew when she caught the smell of the fish and she reached up and patted her paw at Scarlett's leg hopefully.

"Come on then," Abbie coaxed and the two girls scurried out of the station with the kitten at their heels.

"Mum, can we just stay and play with Whiskers for a bit?" Scarlett said when they'd caught up, holding the sandwich behind her back. "I'll bring Abbie to ours in a minute."

Scarlett's mum looked doubtful but then she glanced up the road – their house wasn't far. "What do you think?" she asked Abbie's mum.

"Abbie loves that kitten," her mum sighed. "It's fine with me. Just for a couple of minutes, Abbie!"

Abbie grinned at Scarlett as they watched their mums head off.

Scarlett's mum was making funny faces at baby Jonas.

"Your mum's really nice, asking us over like that. Moving is tough for my mum too. Ooooh, look at Whiskers!"

The tortoiseshell kitten was so excited about the sandwich that she was now trying to climb up Scarlett's leg.

Scarlett laughed. "Sorry! Here you go, Whiskers." She broke off a little piece of sandwich and crouched down to feed her. Then she handed some to Abbie too.

"Thanks! Oh, wow, she really likes it, doesn't she? I suppose cats do love fish."

The two girls took turns to feed Whiskers the tuna sandwich – it was a bit soggy and squished but the kitten didn't seem to care. She ate the whole thing, which was impressive, given how small she was. Then she sat there between them, thoroughly washing her face and looking smug.

"You are a bit fishy," Scarlett told her. "It's all over your whiskers as well... Whiskers is such a good name for her," she said to Abbie. "I love the way she's got different colours on each side of her face. She's really special."

Whiskers swiped a paw over her muzzle, and then stuck out her long, bright pink tongue as far as she could to lick her whiskers. There were still little bits of fish stuck to them, and she didn't want to miss any. She leaned over to sniff thoughtfully at Scarlett and Abbie. They still smelled of fish but perhaps it was just that the scent lingered...

"There's no more," Scarlett told her, showing empty hands. "Are you still hungry?"

Whiskers gave a huge yawn, showing tiny, needlepoint teeth, and a girl passing by laughed and snapped a photo with her phone. "That's the best one yet." She smiled at Scarlett and Abbie, and added, "I've got so many photos of her now. She's so cute, isn't she? I've been putting them on Instagram – everyone loves her." The girl showed them her phone, with loads of beautiful photos of Whiskers mixed in with selfies and pics with friends.

Whiskers got up and strolled over to the girl, rubbing herself around her feet. "Oh, you remembered me! You're such a sweetie," the girl murmured, leaning down to scratch under her chin.

"Her name's Whiskers," Abbie said and the girl nodded.

"I love it. Whiskers the railway kitten."

Knowing she was being talked about, Whiskers stalked over to a patch of warm sunlight and flopped down on the pavement, rolling around on her back with her paws in the air. She was full and sleepy and she wanted her tummy tickled.

"Oh, just look at her!" the girl laughed and took another photo, and then all three of them crouched down to stroke the kitten. Whiskers wriggled blissfully and started to purr.

Chapter Three

"It's nice to see you two getting on so well," Mr Akuffo said. Scarlett and Abbie's teacher was on lunch duty in the hall and he'd just walked past their table.

Scarlett and Abbie smiled at each other, feeling a bit embarrassed. "We both get the same train to school," Scarlett explained.

"We get on at Parson Road," Abbie said, nodding. "Thanks for letting me move tables to sit with Scarlett…"

"Mr Akuffo, did you know there's a railway kitten at Parson Road?" Scarlett put in.

"What, living at the station?" Mr Akuffo looked intrigued. "That's unusual."

"She's got an actual house as well, next door to Abbie," Scarlett told him. "But she likes the station because everyone fusses over her there. She's *really* sweet."

"What does she look like?" Mr Akuffo pulled out his phone and showed them a picture of an enormous, long-haired grey cat. "That's my Billy."

"Wow. He's gorgeous. And about six times the size of Whiskers," Scarlett said. "She's only tiny. She's a tortoiseshell – half her face is ginger with white whiskers and half is brownish-black with black whiskers."

"I've never seen another cat who looks like her," Abbie added. "She's really unusual."

"Sounds like she's pretty special," Mr Akuffo agreed. "And lucky she's got everyone at the station looking out for her. Eat up your lunch, girls, I've kept you chatting too long."

He headed off to check up on a group of noisy Year Fours on the other side of the hall and Scarlett and Abbie went back to their sandwiches. Scarlett had carefully saved some of the ham from hers, since they'd found Whiskers liked ham almost as much as she liked tuna. They couldn't give the kitten too much of it though, because ham was a bit salty for cats.

Scarlett had borrowed Mum's laptop to look up what types of food were safe for cats to eat, in case there was anything they shouldn't be giving her. There was a scarily long list of things – apparently onions were really dangerous, raisins were bad and even dairy foods like cheese and milk could give some cats a stomach upset. No one seemed to have told cats that cheese was bad for them though. Abbie said that when Whiskers climbed in through the window the other day, she'd acted like cheese was the best thing she'd ever tasted.

Scarlett tucked the ham away carefully and went back to what they'd been talking about before Mr Akuffo showed up. "I think we'd be fine getting the train by ourselves."

"I'm still not sure if they'd let us," Abbie said, frowning doubtfully at Scarlett over her apple.

"Well, we could ask!" Scarlett said. "I think my mum would be OK with it. She's always rushing to get us out of the door on time – Poppy eats her breakfast so slowly. If it was just me going to school, it would be a lot easier."

Abbie looked thoughtful. "Yeah… My mum said yesterday that Jonas always wants her to feed him just when she has to collect me from school. OK! Let's ask when they pick us up."

At the end of the day, they hurried out of class to find their mums chatting in the playground. Abbie nudged Scarlett and Scarlett nodded at her and said quickly, "We've been thinking… Can we start going to school on our own? I mean, the two of us would go together but you wouldn't have to come too?"

Both mums looked surprised and a bit doubtful to begin with. Then Scarlett's mum frowned thoughtfully and looked over at Abbie's mum. "I suppose it could be a good idea," she murmured. "When you go to secondary school you'll have to get the train by yourself then – I'll be taking Poppy to nursery at the same time. But – I'm just not sure…"

"We're really sensible," Scarlett pleaded. "You know we are. And the only road we'd have to cross is the one just before school and there's a lollipop lady."

"It would be nice not to have to take Jonas out so early…" Abbie's mum said. "I had to wake him up this morning – he was really grumpy." She rocked Jonas gently in his sling and nibbled her bottom lip.

"We could just try it," Scarlett said. "You can always go back to taking us if it doesn't work out."

"What if you lose your travel card?" Scarlett's mum said.

"We wouldn't!"

"We'll take care of them, we promise." Abbie nodded eagerly. "And I've got my phone now, so we could always call you if there was a problem. We're both ten – that's double figures! We're old enough."

Both mums rolled their eyes at each

other and sighed. "All right then," Scarlett's mum agreed and Scarlett hugged her and then Abbie and then Abbie's mum – carefully so as not to squash Jonas.

"I'll call for you tomorrow!" she told Abbie excitedly. "See you in the morning!"

Travelling to school and back by themselves felt so grown up – Scarlett loved the fact that her mum and dad trusted her. And it meant that if she and Abbie got themselves organized and left early enough, they could spend a little bit longer fussing over Whiskers at the station.

That first morning, they were so early they had time to sit on one of the benches to wait for the train. Whiskers hopped up beside them and stomped up and down between their laps as though she wasn't sure which

girl she liked best, purring all the time. The kitten was definitely getting friendlier every day – so many people stopped to say hello and stroke her as they walked along the platform.

"I don't know how you purr so loudly when you're so little," Scarlett said, running her hand along the kitten's silky back. Whiskers butted her head up against Scarlett's hand, eyes closed, and purred even louder, if that was possible. Then she padded her paws into Scarlett's school skirt, flexing tiny claws in and out of the fabric, and lay down. She looked like a tiny statue, her front paws stretched out as she watched the station platform – almost as if it belonged to her.

"That cat's running this station," one of the staff said, laughing as he walked past. "She's taking notes."

Abbie giggled and Scarlett smiled at the man. He was right – Whiskers did look as though she was watching to make sure everything was running smoothly. The railway kitten was most definitely in charge.

Scarlett rang the doorbell for Abbie's flat and leaned against the wall, looking around to see if she could spot Whiskers. The kitten spent a lot of her time at the station but they did sometimes see her sitting on the wall next door or prowling around the little front garden.

"Hello!" Abbie flung the door open and Scarlett grinned at her.

They hurried along the road to the station and through the ticket hall to the platform. Scarlett was expecting

Whiskers to dash up to them the way she usually did – the kitten's throaty purr always made her laugh. But today there was no kitten galloping along the platform.

"Maybe she's in the ticket hall and we missed her?" Abbie said, frowning, and they went back to the barriers to look.

"Haven't seen her this morning, girls!" Lucy, one of the station staff, called over. "Never mind. You'll catch her on the way back from school."

Scarlett and Abbie nodded and waved goodbye to Lucy but it felt weird walking back out on to the platform to wait for the train. They hardly ever waited there without Whiskers.

"Hey, where's the kitten?" a girl asked as she went past.

"She's not around this morning," Scarlett said, shrugging. She was trying to convince herself that it was OK, that Whiskers was just off exploring somewhere else, but there was a little niggling lump of worry inside her. Where *was* she?

"Maybe Whiskers is just at her house," Abbie said. "I mean, she does live there, doesn't she?"

"Yeah…" Scarlett wrapped her arms around her middle, trying to squeeze

47

the worried lump away. "Yes. You're right. I suppose we're always saying they don't look after their kitten properly…"

"And now we're upset because they are," Abbie agreed. "Oh well." She glanced down the tracks. "I think I can see the train."

The speakers crackled overhead announcing that the train was coming and the girls joined the crowd getting ready to board. The train was already busy when it arrived and Scarlett was pressed against the doors. She peered out of the window as the train pulled away from the station, desperately hoping for just a glimpse of the little kitten – but the platform was empty.

Whiskers twitched, shivered and let out a silent mew. She hurt all over. What had happened? Where was she? She couldn't remember anything. The kitten tried to mew again but only a breathy little squeak came out.

She was lying on the ground – some rough, cold surface. It was damp as well and she felt frozen all the way through. A car rumbled past and the kitten shuddered with fear. That had been close – too close.

A car...

There had been a car...

Something had been moving on the other side of the road, in the darkness. Whiskers hadn't known what it was – another cat, maybe? A bird? She'd wanted to see... She hadn't been thinking about cars, the road was quiet. But then, all of a sudden the car had been there, huge and loud. And after that she didn't remember what had happened, all she knew was that everything hurt.

Was she still in the road? Whiskers tried to raise her head and look around, her breathing suddenly fast with panic. She could just see ... she was at the edge of the road. Not right in the middle but not safe either. She had to move. Slowly, painfully, the kitten scrabbled against the tarmac, dragging herself out of danger. She was waking up a little more now and she could tell that it wasn't truly everything that hurt. She felt bruised and shaky but it was her back leg that was really painful. Whiskers couldn't make it move at all and it was trailing out behind her as she crawled along.

She just had to get out of the road before any more cars came roaring by. Only a little further and she'd be safe and hidden under that parked car. A stone bumped against her injured leg and Whiskers mewed miserably. But she was almost there. Exhausted, the kitten wriggled into the safe shadows under the car. She slumped down, dazed, and closed her eyes. She just needed to rest…

Chapter Four

Scarlett and Abbie were almost silent on the train on the way home from school. Scarlett said, "I'm sure we'll see Whiskers when we get off the train," and Abbie nodded and said, "Definitely." But that was it. They just weren't in the mood to talk.

When they stepped off the train, they looked at each other for a moment and Scarlett swallowed, trying to get rid of that nervous feeling inside her. It had kept coming back all day.

"She'll be there," Abbie said but Scarlett could tell she wasn't as confident as she was trying to sound. Neither of them started walking along the platform towards the stairs. Not yet.

The train pulled slowly out of the station, which meant they could see across the tracks to the opposite platform. Scarlett had hoped to see the tortoiseshell kitten staring back at them – perhaps perched on her favourite bench.

"I can't see her," she said, anxiously scanning the platform. "Can you?"

Abbie was silent for a moment while she searched too and then she sighed. "No. But she could be out at the front. Or sitting on her garden wall. Come on."

They hurried up the stairs and along the footbridge, then down to the other 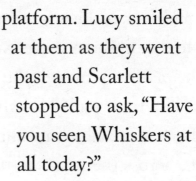 platform. Lucy smiled at them as they went past and Scarlett stopped to ask, "Have you seen Whiskers at all today?"

Lucy frowned. "No ... no, I haven't," she said slowly. "You were looking for her this morning, weren't you?"

"She wasn't there," Scarlett murmured.

"That's all day, then."

"I expect she's just at home," Lucy said reassuringly. "It's a bit chilly today – she's probably curled up indoors in the warm!"

Abbie and Scarlett exchanged a look. They hoped so too – but neither of them quite believed it.

"Shall we go and knock at the house next door and ask if she's there?" Abbie asked, chewing her bottom lip as they stood outside the station.

Scarlett looked down the road at the houses. "I know it's only been a day – but it's not like her, is it? We should probably check. Do you think they'll be home?"

"I don't know." Abbie shook her

head. "We don't see them very often, I think they both work long hours. We can try though."

They started walking along the road – faster now that they'd made a decision. But then Scarlett grabbed her friend's arm.

"Wait a minute, Abbie. What's that?" She pointed into the road – at something underneath one of the parked cars. A little pile of dark patched fur.

"Oh no!" Abbie whispered and then she added, "Be careful!" as Scarlett crouched down to get a closer look.

"It's her." Scarlett's voice was shaking. "It's Whiskers. I think she's been hit by a car."

"Is she – is she badly hurt? What should we do?" Abbie asked, looking around for someone to help them. There were people hurrying along the road from the station but they didn't know any of them and no one stopped to ask if there was something wrong.

Scarlett stared at Whiskers – she was so still and her eyes were closed but she could see … yes, the dark fur was moving up and down just a little. She was breathing! Scarlett shrugged off her backpack, undid her school cardigan and laid it on the road next to Whiskers.

"Are you going to pick her up?" Abbie said nervously. "What if it hurts her?"

"I know, but we can't leave her here. We need to get her to your neighbours so they can take her to the vet." Scarlett sucked in a breath. She was scared to touch Whiskers – she looked so small and fragile – what if picking her up made things worse? But someone was going to have to move her. She slid both hands underneath the kitten and lifted her on to the cardigan. Whiskers was limp but she hissed as Scarlett laid her down. The kitten opened her eyes and looked up at them in a daze.

"It's going to be OK," Scarlett told her, trying to sound loving and gentle and reassuring instead of terrified. "We're getting help. Oh, Whiskers, it'll be OK…"

"I'll go and tell them." Abbie ran on ahead but by the time Scarlett caught up she was turning away from her neighbours' door. "No one's answering – I don't think they're home. I'm going to get my mum."

"OK." Scarlett nodded. "The vet's is on the high street, it's not far. We could just take her round there." She looked down at Whiskers, huddled up in the cardigan. She was so little and light to carry. But the kitten was awake and she did seem to be looking up at her. That had to be a good sign, right?

Where was Abbie? Scarlett looked over her shoulder, wondering if she should just go to the vet's on her own. But then Abbie came out of her door, with her mum tucking Jonas into the sling on her front.

"Lara, can you come with us to the

vet? Please?" Scarlett burst out. She held out her bundle of cardigan and Abbie's mum looked anxiously at the kitten.

"Of course I will. Poor little thing. I suppose she ran out into the road."

Scarlett swallowed and nodded, and Abbie's mum put an arm round her shoulders.

They were lucky to live so close to the vet's, Scarlett realized, as they hurried round the corner. Abbie's mum didn't have a car and Scarlett's dad had gone to work in theirs.

There was no one in the waiting room when they dashed in, only the vet nurse, who smiled at them all and then noticed Whiskers in Scarlett's arms. He leaned across to the door behind him and called urgently, "Anna!" and then turned back to Scarlett and Abbie and Abbie's mum. "The vet's just coming."

"Oh, Scarlett, don't cry," Abbie's mum said gently. "They're going to help."

"I know, I'm trying not to," Scarlett sniffed. But now that Whiskers was in the right place and someone was going to look after her, she just couldn't stop.

A vet in dark green scrubs led them into the back of the surgery and helped Scarlett lay Whiskers down on a tall examining table, still wrapped in the cardigan.

"Was it a car?" the vet asked as she felt gently down Whiskers' legs.

"We don't know for sure," Scarlett said, looking at Abbie. "But we found her at the edge of the road so I suppose it must have been. She wasn't very far from her house."

"Oh, is she not yours?" the vet looked up, surprised.

"No, she belongs to our next-door neighbours," Abbie's mum explained. "They're out and I don't have a number for them."

"We know she's called Whiskers though," Scarlett put in. "We made friends with her at the station. She's always there…"

Whiskers let out a pained mew and the vet murmured soothingly to her. "Sorry, little one." She looked up. "I'm going to have to do some X-rays. This could just be a bad sprain but I think it's more likely that her back leg's broken."

"But – can you mend it?" Scarlett burst out. "Put it in plaster or something? She'll be OK, won't she?"

The vet glanced at her and smiled but she seemed worried. "We'll keep her comfortable. But we need to get hold of her owners as soon as we can."

64

Whiskers twitched
as she caught
the strange
new smell. It
was so sharp
and strong that it
made her nose itch, and she huddled
back into Scarlett's cardigan. It smelled
of Scarlett – she knew that scent and
it was comforting. She needed the
comfort just then.

Someone was touching her now,
pressing against her ribs and feeling
along her stomach. She hissed, trying
to pull away, but the person wouldn't
let her.

"It's OK, Whiskers."

The kitten looked up and saw Scarlett
leaning over her anxiously, and Abbie

65

too. They were here in this strange place, people she knew… That helped. Whiskers wriggled, trying to get away from the fingers now gently feeling around her damaged leg. She wanted to get to Scarlett – she *trusted* Scarlett. Scarlett fed her but it wasn't just that. Whiskers was hurt and she needed help and Scarlett made her feel safe.

The kitten mewed hopefully but she couldn't wriggle out of the cardigan – she was still feeling so wobbly and her paws were all tangled. She could see Scarlett but she couldn't reach her.

Someone was lifting her up and carrying her away. Whiskers mewed again, wanting to go back – but Scarlett was gone.

Chapter Five

The vet sent Scarlett, Abbie and Abbie's mum out to sit in the waiting room while she had a closer look at Whiskers. They sat silently on the chairs, listening to Jonas grizzle – he'd woken up and he was hungry.

"I'd better text your mum and let her know what's happening," Abbie's mum said suddenly. "Oh wow. I didn't realize how long we'd been here… I hope she's not worrying too much."

Scarlett pulled her phone out of the bottom of her bag – it was an old one of Dad's that he'd given her when she and Abbie started travelling on their own, just in case there were any problems. It wasn't very fancy, mostly it just did calls and texts, but it was enough – and there were two missed calls and three texts from Mum already.

"I should have sent her a message," Scarlett said. "I didn't even think…"

"Never mind. I'm sure she'll understand," Abbie's mum said comfortingly. "There. I've sent it."

"The vet's coming back," Abbie whispered, nodding towards the door.

Anna came round the reception

desk to talk to them all. She looked worried.

"Is her leg broken?" Scarlett burst out. "Is Whiskers going to be OK?"

Anna took a deep breath. "There's good news and bad news," she explained carefully. "I think Whiskers does have a broken leg. But she's breathing well and she's quite calm and stable. That means it's unlikely she's got any internal injuries – damage to her kidneys or anything like that. But we need to do X-rays to find out exactly what's going on with her leg. Depending on what sort of break it is, she could need an operation to pin the bone. That's something which she'll need a specialist vet for. And I'm sorry to say this – even just the X-rays are going to cost a lot but if she does need an operation, it'll be expensive."

Abbie's mum's face fell. "When you say expensive…"

Anna sighed. "Probably thousands of pounds."

Scarlett and Abbie gaped at her. Scarlett had never imagined mending Whiskers could cost that much. It was a fortune.

"We really need to get in touch with her owner," Anna explained. "We can't treat Whiskers without their permission, you see. She's resting comfortably out the back at the moment. We've given her something for the pain but that's all we can do right now."

"We'll go and see if they're home," Abbie's mum said, looking worried. "I suppose we can put a note through the door. Oh wow. OK. We'll be in touch as soon we can."

"Thank you for looking after Whiskers," Scarlett whispered and Anna smiled at her.

"She's lovely. You can tell she's friendly, even when she's hurting. We're taking good care of her."

"Mum, what if the people next door can't pay that much money for Whiskers?" Abbie asked shakily as they walked back along the high street.

"I don't know." Abbie's mum shook her head. "Sorry, girls. I just don't know."

Dad met Scarlett at the door with a massive hug. "There you are! Scarlett, we were really worried about you. Mum didn't know where you were."

"Sorry." Scarlett sniffed. She leaned against her dad and wrapped her arms tight around his waist. Then she looked round the side of him to see Mum hurrying out of the kitchen, carrying Poppy. "Sorry, Mum."

"Oh, Scarlett. It's not that we're cross. Not really anyway, you just had us worried. What happened at the vet's? How's Whiskers?"

"Her leg might be broken. The vet thinks it is, but she can't tell for sure till they've done X-rays. But it's going to cost loads to fix. Maybe thousands." Scarlett pressed her face into her dad's T-shirt. "I don't know if Abbie's neighbours can pay that. Abbie says they're never around to look after her. They don't have a cat flap and Whiskers is at the station all the time because she can't get into their house. I don't even think they feed her enough!" she added in a wail.

"Don't jump to conclusions, Scarlett," Dad said gently. "We don't know what's

73

going to happen. And at least Whiskers is in the right place."

Mum nodded. "From what Lara said, it sounds like it was lucky you spotted her."

"She's such a sweet kitten," Dad said. "I saw her outside the station a couple of days ago and she was really friendly." He sighed. "Perhaps her leg's not broken after all. It might not cost too much."

"Maybe…" Scarlett said but she could tell that Dad wasn't very hopeful either.

Whiskers peered through the thin wire bars at the front of the cage. Where had Scarlett and Abbie gone? It had been Scarlett who'd wrapped her up

in the warm cardigan but now she'd
disappeared and left her in this strange
place. The light was too bright and
she could hear other animals moving
around – another cat, she thought,
somewhere on the far side of the room.
She'd heard a mew. The cat sounded as
confused and lonely as she was.

"Hey…" The voice was gentle but
Whiskers still flinched away. She
didn't trust anyone here, not yet. The
person who'd spoken moved towards
her slowly and opened the front of
the cage. "It's all right, little one. Just
bringing you some more blankets to
lie on. And this, look." He slipped
a padded fleece into the cage and
arranged it carefully while Whiskers
watched him. The kitten was pressed

as far back against the wall of the cage as she could manage, which wasn't that far – it still hurt to move her leg, though not as much as it had before.

"There, you see – it's a shelter – you can snuggle inside there now, if you're scared." He sighed. "No one's managed to get in touch with your owner yet. We're not going to be able to do anything about your leg until tomorrow. You just stay there and rest, all right? We're doing our best for you, kitten."

Whiskers glared at him suspiciously but his soft voice and slow, quiet movements were helping her feel calmer. She didn't like it here, not at all, but she thought perhaps this person was kind.

She was tired again. Her leg was aching but it felt strange and far away – as though it wasn't really hurting as much as it should. Wearily, she wriggled so that she was half under the sleeve of Scarlett's cardigan. The fabric was soft and warm and it smelled like Scarlett. Whiskers let out a shuddery breath and closed her eyes. Maybe when she woke up, Scarlett would come and find her.

Scarlett rang Abbie's doorbell and stood there on the step, her heart thumping. Lara had messaged Mum last night, saying they'd managed to get hold of their neighbours at last. The neighbours had said they would contact the vet but Scarlett hadn't heard anything since then.

Scarlett's mum wouldn't let her leave to go and meet Abbie any earlier than usual – she said it wasn't fair when Lara would be busy getting Abbie and Jonas up – but Scarlett had been sitting there waiting to go for ages.

Abbie opened the front door and Scarlett could see at once that it wasn't good news. Her friend's eyes were red, as though she'd been crying.

"What's going on?"

Abbie stepped out and pulled the door closed behind her. "They can't pay for it," she said dully as they started walking towards the station. "Not even for Whiskers to have an X-ray."

"But – but then what's going to happen?" Scarlett stared at her. And then she realized what it meant. *That* was why Abbie had been crying. "Are they going to tell the vet to put her to sleep?" she whispered.

Abbie nodded. "That's what they said. Dan – that's the man next door – he texted Mum to say thank you for helping but there was nothing they could do. He said they were really sad about it."

"She's only a kitten!" Scarlett burst out. "They can't have her put down, she's so little!"

"I know," Abbie said miserably. "I asked Mum if we could help and she said she wished we could but it's just so much money."

Scarlett swallowed. Dad had said how sweet Whiskers was, and Mum loved her – even Poppy did. But a big, expensive operation… All that money needed at once. There was no way her parents would be able to afford it either.

But – did they need to?

Scarlett grabbed hold of Abbie's arm, pulling her to a stop. "What if we could get the money?" she demanded.

"How?" Abbie blinked at her. "Where are we going to get that much?"

"We could raise it! Like a charity thing – my cousin raised more than two thousand pounds last year. Her school was running this special trip and she had to do loads of fundraising. She did all sorts – a dance marathon, a car wash. Cake sales. Couldn't we do stuff like that?"

"OK, but it takes ages," Abbie pointed out. "We need the money *now*."

Scarlett nodded. "I suppose… Unless…" Her eyes widened. "Abbie, come with me." She whisked round, pulling Abbie after her.

"But we've got to get to school! Scarlett, you're going the wrong way!"

"We're not going to the station," Scarlett said grimly. "We're going to talk to the vet. Now." She glanced round at Abbie. "We have to, don't you see? We've got to tell them we're going to get the money. We can't wait until after school. It might be too late."

Abbie started walking faster. "You mean … by then Whiskers might already have been put down?"

Chapter Six

Scarlett knocked on the glass door at the front of the vet's. She could see the vet nurse they'd met the day before looking at the computer behind the reception desk but the door was locked.

"Oh, please..." she whispered, waving at him as he looked up.

He seemed to remember who they

were because he smiled and came round the desk towards them. He unlocked the door and stood there eyeing them curiously.

"Hey. Are you OK? Can I help with something? You were the ones who brought in the little tortoiseshell kitten, right?"

Scarlett looked at Abbie, suddenly unsure what to say. How were they going to explain what they wanted?

"Whiskers is doing all right. We gave her some painkillers and she's pretty comfortable." The vet nurse smiled at them reassuringly but then he looked out into the street as though he was expecting to see an adult with them. "Um, shouldn't you two be on your way to school?"

"We are. We – we just needed to come here first." Scarlett crossed her fingers behind her back and took a deep breath. "We have plenty of time, don't worry. The thing is – Abbie's neighbours said they can't pay for Whiskers to be treated. So – we've come to ask – please could you get her leg better and *we'll* pay you? But not right now..." She swallowed, glancing at Abbie for help.

"We're going to raise the money," Abbie put in. "And we know it's going to be a lot. We just need some time, that's all. We've got lots of ideas."

"But Whiskers can't wait for us to raise the money," Scarlett said pleadingly.

"Oh, I see…" The nurse – it said Sean on his name tag – was nodding now, a thoughtful look on his face. "That's a really kind thing to do."

"We mean it," Scarlett told him. "We – we were worried that you might put Whiskers to sleep. That's why we came here now … in case after school was too late," she added, in a smaller voice.

"We're doing our absolute best not to let that happen," Sean said gently. "The vet's actually done the X-rays already. We've got an arrangement with a local charity, you see. They are funding some of the treatment. Whiskers is really young and healthy, and we want to get her sorted out."

Scarlett felt like hugging him. "You mean, it's all going to be OK?" she asked huskily. "The charity's going to pay for her?"

Sean made a face. "Not quite. We've been trying to work out what to do. The X-rays showed that her leg's badly broken. She's going to need an operation to fix it – a complicated one that's going to have to be done by a specialist. They need to put a frame on her leg to hold the broken bone in place. Anna and Mike – they're the vets – they don't think the charity fund's going to be able to cover the whole cost."

"That's what Anna meant yesterday, when she said it might be really expensive..." Scarlett sighed. She'd been so hopeful for a moment and then that hope had been whipped away. "What about our idea though? Can you do the operation and we promise we'll raise the money?"

Sean held up his hands. "I'm not sure – I think it's a great idea but it's not up to me. Give me a minute, OK?" He disappeared into the back of the clinic, leaving Scarlett and Abbie looking at each other worriedly.

"What do you think they'll say?" Abbie whispered.

"I don't know." Scarlett leaned

wearily against the reception desk. "I suppose they *might* do it, if they believe we can get the money." Now that they weren't caught up in a wild rush to save Whiskers, Scarlett wasn't absolutely sure whether she believed they could do it either.

But we have to, she told herself. *We will.*

"Hello." Anna, the same vet from the day before, came back out with Sean. "I love your idea, girls."

Scarlett glanced at Abbie. It really sounded as though Anna was about to say, *But. But we can't help. But it's too much money. But we can't risk it…*

"I've been phoning around and I think we can probably scrape together some more money – the shelter we

do some voluntary work for also says
they can help. It's going to be tight
but I think we have enough to give
Whiskers the treatment."

Scarlett nodded eagerly.

"But if you can raise some money
too – well, that would be brilliant."
Anna smiled at them. "It will mean
the shelter can use their funds to help
another animal, won't it?"

"We will," Scarlett promised, her
voice squeaky with relief. She wanted
to give Anna a hug but she held herself
back. "Will Whiskers be OK, once
she's had the operation? I mean, her
leg's not so bad that she won't be able
to walk properly again?"

"I expect she'll be fine. There are
always risks with an operation but

cats do break their legs quite often
and they usually heal really well.
Especially when they're young like
Whiskers. And there are things we
can do to help too, if we've got more
funds to spend on her. Like organize
some physiotherapy to get her moving
again if she's struggling." Anna's smile
widened. "She's feeling a bit sorry for
herself at the moment. Would you like
to see if you can cheer her up?"

Whiskers heard the click of the door latch and footsteps. Her whiskers twitched and her ears flattened but only a little. She wasn't quite as scared as she had been the night before, but she still didn't like it here. She wanted to be back at the station, being fussed over by the people hurrying past, without the dull ache in her leg and the strange dizzy feeling. But everyone who'd fed her and handled her in this sharp-smelling room had been kind. So she peered cautiously out of her cardigan nest instead of trying to huddle and hide away.

"You've got visitors, Whiskers." Anna unlatched the door of the cage and opened it carefully. She was shielding the gap with her hand but Whiskers didn't want to leap out anyway. She was still groggy and exhausted, and she didn't feel like moving. "Can you see them?" Anna asked her, moving over a little.

It was Scarlett and Abbie!

Whiskers mewed loudly and tried to hop up on to three legs to get closer to them but Anna gently blocked her. "Hey, little one. Don't hurt yourself. Scarlett, Abbie – if you come a bit closer then she won't have to move to get to you. There, that's it."

Whiskers wobbled forwards, nudging her chin into Scarlett's hand. They were here, at last. People she knew, people she loved – and that she knew loved her.

"Oh, Whiskers, we were worried about you," Scarlett whispered. "You look so tiny in that cage."

Scarlett's voice was shaking. Whiskers licked Scarlett's fingers and then rubbed the side of her face against Abbie's sleeve. She leaned lovingly against them both, feeling safer than she had since that awful moment when she'd woken up on the road.

Very, very faintly, she began to purr.

Chapter Seven

"We should let her rest again," Anna said gently, smiling at Abbie and Scarlett. "We need to be careful with her."

"I suppose…" Scarlett said, looking sadly at the cage. It was very bare and miserable looking, even with her red cardigan and the fleecy cat cave brightening it up. She didn't want to leave Whiskers behind. Although she knew it was the best place for her right now, the kitten looked so small and lonely.

A tiny mew sounded behind them, just as she and Abbie reached the door. Scarlett looked round, wanting to run back to her, but Anna was already shepherding them into the waiting room.

Sean leaned over the reception desk and waved at them. "I hate to mention it but you two are definitely going to be late for school."

Scarlett and Abbie stared at each other for a moment. They'd completely forgotten about school. Scarlett glanced at the clock on the wall behind Sean and swallowed. They'd missed their usual train by miles.

"We've got to get to the station," Abbie gasped.

"Good luck – and if you need someone to talk to the school and explain, get them to call us, all right?" Sean looked worried. "Will you be OK getting there? Should I get in touch with your parents or something?"

"We get the train every day, don't worry!" Scarlett called back as they dashed out of the door.

"We're going to be so late," Abbie wheezed as they pelted down the road, dodging people out doing their shopping.

"There's a train in about two minutes, isn't there?" Scarlett said. "We *might* make it…"

They raced into the station just as

the train was pulling in and started fumbling for their tickets.

"It's OK, girls." Lucy waved at them and used her pass to open the barriers. "I was thinking I hadn't seen you this morning! Are you OK?"

"Whiskers is at the vet's! She got hit by a car!" Scarlett called as they darted through the barriers.

Lucy looked horrified and Scarlett yelled, "She's going to be all right! We'll tell you about it later!" as they jumped on to the train just before the doors closed.

They'd got on after everybody else so they were stuck close to the door but at least they were on the train. "We'll only be a bit late," Abbie said hopefully and Scarlett nodded.

"Maybe Mr Akuffo will be slow doing the register, if he's got chatting about a book or something," she suggested. They might be lucky. She really didn't want school ringing Mum, not after her parents had explained how worried they'd been the day before.

"Are you two OK?"

Scarlett and Abbie looked round,

surprised, and saw that there was a girl standing behind them – the girl they'd talked to at the station a few days ago, the one who'd taken loads of cute photos of Whiskers.

"I thought maybe I was magically early but you're late… Sorry – I'm Alexa, do you remember me? I talked to you about the railway kitten." She grinned at them, shrugging. "Did you miss your train?"

"Yeah…" Scarlett sighed. "We were at the vet's, with Whiskers."

Alexa stopped smiling. "The kitten? Why, what's wrong with her?"

"She got hit by a car," Scarlett explained. "Her leg's broken. We found her on the road outside the station yesterday afternoon."

"Oh no!" Alexa sounded really shocked. "That's awful."

"And her owners can't pay for the operation to mend it," Abbie put in. "The vet's have got a charity helping them with her but we need to raise some more money to make sure they can do everything she needs."

"If it wasn't for that charity she might have been put down." Scarlett swallowed. "But they might not be able to cover everything – like if she needs help to walk again afterwards. And we don't want to use all their funds or they won't be able to help any other animals."

Alexa nodded. "Yeah, definitely. Poor little cat. That must have been really scary for you finding her too. So are you going to set up a crowdfunder then?"

Scarlett glanced at Abbie uncertainly. She wasn't exactly sure what a crowdfunder was – although it sounded like a good thing.

"It's like a special fund you set up online and get people to donate to," Alexa added. "You should ask someone at home to look up how to do it. I bet lots of people would want to help Whiskers. She's really popular with everyone who comes through the station. I sent her picture to a website all about cats with jobs too and loads of people commented how cute she was. You could put it on all the local social media accounts."

"And maybe they'd let us put up posters at the station?" Abbie said hopefully.

"Yes, exactly!" Alexa glanced up. "Look – we're coming into your station.

You'd better run!"

"Thanks for the idea!" Scarlett said as she and Abbie grabbed their bags. "We'll let you know what happens with Whiskers!"

"I'll donate to your fund!" Alexa called as they jumped down from the train. "Good luck!"

They weren't so late that the playground gates were shut but they had to buzz the front doors and get let in by Mrs Ryan in the office.

"What happened to you two? Problems with the trains? Never mind, you're here now. I'll mark down that you're in." She waved them on into school and Scarlett and Abbie decided it was probably easier not to explain. At least it sounded as if she hadn't had time to call their parents yet and check where they'd got to.

They sneaked into the Year Five classroom trying to look as well-behaved and apologetic as possible.

"Did Mrs Ryan sign you in?" Mr Akuffo called, turning round from the board, and Scarlett and Abbie chorused, "Yes!"

"OK." Mr Akuffo went on explaining the morning literacy task – writing a letter from the point of view of one of the characters in their class book – but when he'd finished he came over to their table.

"Was your train late, then?"

"No…" Scarlett took a deep breath. Mr Akuffo had that beautiful cat, Billy. He'd understand that they'd had to do their best to help Whiskers. "We're late because we went to the vet clinic near us. You know we told you about the kitten at Parson Road station?"

Mr Akuffo nodded.

"She got run over yesterday. Actually, we don't know when it happened, we found her under a car on the way home from school."

"Oh, Scarlett, I'm really sorry to hear that. How is she?" Mr Akuffo crouched down by the table, looking worried.

Scarlett explained to him about the broken leg and the scary amount of money it was going to cost to put right. "Abbie found out this morning that her neighbours can't pay for it," she explained. "We were scared that the vet would have to put Whiskers to sleep. So we went to ask them if we could pay for her instead."

"Mr Akuffo, do you know what a crowdfunder is?" Abbie asked. "A girl we know on the train said we should set one up for Whiskers. We were thinking of having a cake sale too."

"Yes, a crowdfunder's a way to

raise money – but hang on, girls – do you mean you were late because you went to the vet's instead of coming to school? You went there on your own? Not with your parents?"

Scarlett chewed her bottom lip and looked worriedly at Abbie. "Um… Yes?"

Mr Akuffo sighed. "Right."

"The vet nurse said you could ring him and he'd explain!" Scarlett added quickly. "It's Parson Road Animal Clinic."

"Sounds like I'd better do that at break," Mr Akuffo said slowly – but he sounded more worried than cross.

By break time, Scarlett was wondering if Mr Akuffo was going to tell their parents they shouldn't be allowed to go on the train on their own ever again. He'd looked so concerned earlier on. She really didn't want her mum and dad to be upset, not after yesterday. Would they understand how she and Abbie had felt about Whiskers? How scared they'd been that the vet might have to put her to sleep?

"It'll be OK," Abbie whispered as the bell went. "Sean at the vet's was nice. He'll explain to Mr Akuffo."

"I'm more worried about my mum," Scarlett said gloomily.

"Me too." Abbie sighed. "There's nothing we can do about it now though. Look, I've got my felt tips and a drawing pad. We could make posters to put up at the station?"

"Good idea." Scarlett nodded. She

really wanted to do something useful.

They'd already made two beautiful posters with portraits of Whiskers and PLEASE HELP on them in big letters when Mr Akuffo came out to the playground to find them.

"You two owe me," he said, leaning over to look at the posters. "I've calmed down both your mums. Scarlett, your mum's calling the vet clinic to ask for the details of that charity so she can set up a fundraiser online for them."

"Wow!" Scarlett stared at him. She hadn't been expecting him to say that at all.

"I explained that you were really scared about what might happen to Whiskers. But I think you've used up all your chances for ever being more than thirty seconds late home, girls. And Mrs Ryan's going to check with the head but you can probably have a cake sale the week after half-term. Did you know Mrs Ryan's got three cats at home?" He smiled at them. "I couldn't help imagining how I'd feel if something happened to Billy," he admitted. "I'd have forgotten all about my train and run to the vet's as well…"

Chapter Eight

When they arrived back at the station that afternoon, Scarlett and Abbie went to look for Lucy. They found her in the ticket hall with Tony, the man who'd given Scarlett cat treats to feed the kitten.

"I've been looking out for you!" Lucy said eagerly. "I was just telling Tony. What's happened to poor little Whiskers?"

Scarlett and Abbie explained and showed them the posters. "My mum's set up a crowdfunder for Whiskers' treatment," Scarlett told them. "We've just got to add the details on to the posters. Then can we put them up in the station?"

"Definitely." Tony nodded. "We'll point them out to passengers as well. A couple of people have already asked me where the kitten is today."

Scarlett smiled at Abbie, feeling relieved. It did sound as though the crowdfunding idea might work.

"My mum's just texted me to say she's at your house," Abbie told Scarlett, holding up her phone. "We'd better get there before they start worrying."

Scarlett nodded. She knew Mr Akuffo had stuck up for them but she was still worried about her mum and dad being upset with her. Now definitely wasn't the time to be late.

They hurried along the road to Scarlett's and let themselves in. Their mums were drinking tea in the kitchen, Abbie's mum holding Jonas against her hip. Poppy was playing with her toy food under the table.

"Hi, Mum!" Scarlett said, crossing her fingers behind her back, and Abbie gave Lara a hug and kissed Jonas's head.

Scarlett's mum put her coffee cup down and glared at her. "You went off to the vet's on your own!"

Scarlett decided this probably wasn't the time to say that actually she'd been with Abbie. She knew what her mum meant. "It was really important," she pleaded.

Her mum sighed. "You're very lucky you've got Mr Akuffo telling me how well-behaved and sensible you usually are, and that this was an emergency."

"He told me that the two of you are really good in class," Abbie's mum put in. "And that Scarlett's been making Abbie feel very welcome."

Scarlett went pink.

"But you still shouldn't have gone to the vet's on your own!" Scarlett's mum added. "You must have known we wouldn't be happy about that."

Scarlett looked at her feet. "Yes… But we were thinking about Whiskers – and we thought the vet might have to put her to sleep, Mum! We didn't know how much time there was."

"I know." Her mum reached out and put an arm round her. "Did Mr Akuffo tell you I've set up the crowdfunder?"

"Yes! It's brilliant. We told Lucy and Tony at the station and they said we can put up posters about it." Scarlett reached into her school bag to show them to her mum. "Has anyone given any money yet?"

"Well, me," her mum said, smiling.

"And me and your auntie Laurel," Abbie's mum added.

"Let's have a look. But don't be upset if no one's donated. I only set it up a few hours ago, remember." Scarlett's mum opened up her phone. "I did share it on all the local pages too... Oh!" She blinked, surprised, and then turned the phone round so they could all see the screen.

"But that's half of what you said you were aiming for!" Scarlett squeaked. "Already! And we haven't even done the cake sale yet!"

"Yes – I put the absolute most the nurse at the vet's said it would cost and explained that if they didn't need it all for Whiskers it would go to the charity who'd already paid for some of the treatment."

Scarlett grabbed Abbie and they twirled each other round the table – they'd never expected to raise so much money so quickly.

"That's amazing. It just shows how many people love her." Abbie's mum smiled. "Right, Abbie, we'd better head home and get dinner ready."

Abbie nodded. "See you tomorrow! I can't wait to tell Mr Akuffo the news."

"Yeah! I'll write the bit about the crowdfunder on the posters and we can put them up on the way to school," Scarlett suggested.

Once Abbie and her mum had gone, Scarlett read through some of the messages people had left on the site – most of them saying how sweet Whiskers was and how she'd really cheered them up on their daily commute. She was still scrolling through them when the phone started ringing and she handed it back to her mum.

"Hello! Oh, yes, that's me. Great – and she's OK?"

Scarlett hissed, "Is it the vet?" and her mum nodded and put her thumb up. But then she frowned. "Right. Yes, I see. OK. I'll pass that on to the girls, and thank you for letting me know. Just to say, we've already raised half of the money – yes, people have been so generous. Mm-hm. Bye!"

"What is it?" Scarlett begged. "You suddenly looked all worried. What's happened?"

Her mum sighed. "It's good news, don't worry. They did the operation and they've put something called an external fixator on Whiskers' leg. It's like a metal frame that's pinned to her. And she's awake and she's even had something to eat."

"So … why were you looking like that?"

"It's Abbie's neighbours – they say they can't have her back,"Mum said slowly."Whiskers is going to need cage rest because she's not allowed to walk on her broken leg. And that could take a while. Someone needs to be checking on her and they're always out at work. They said they're going to give her to the shelter."

"Oh." Scarlett blinked. "But – what if someone adopts her and they don't live near the station? We won't be able to see her any more." She looked at her mum and then went on slowly, "Actually, that's good, isn't it? If she's got a home where they look after her and she doesn't need to go to the station…"

"Mmmm. But she loves it there now," Mum said thoughtfully. "She belongs. She's the railway kitten! I expect she'd miss it."

"Mum…" Scarlett reached out to put her hand on her mum's arm. "We live close to the station. Whiskers could even walk down there with me and Abbie."

"Scarlett…"

"And it's half-term next week, so I could look after Whiskers then."

Her mum put her head on one side. "And after you're back at school?"

"I suppose I was thinking you're at home *most* of the day," Scarlett

murmured. "Poppy loves Whiskers
too. And Dad said she was cute."

"That doesn't mean he wants to
adopt her!" Scarlett's mum laughed.
"But – maybe. I can't imagine
Whiskers going to the shelter, after all
this. Dad and I will talk about it."

"You will?" Scarlett leaped up and
rushed round the table to give Mum a
hug.

Might they really be able to bring
Whiskers home?

Whiskers pressed her nose against
Scarlett's hand and then rolled on to her
side a little further to show more of her
tummy. Scarlett was certain Whiskers

had missed them. She and Mum and Poppy had been out to get some food for dinner – Abbie was coming over so she could see Whiskers and they were going to make their own pizzas. They'd only been out for about half an hour but Whiskers had started to mew as soon as Mum opened the front door. Loud, bossy mews that clearly meant, *Make a fuss of me now.*

"Be careful," Scarlett cooed soothingly as she stroked the silky ginger and black fur. "Don't hurt your leg." She was reaching carefully into the crate the vet had lent them. It seemed tiny – it fitted on to the edge of the kitchen counter – but Anna had explained that Whiskers really mustn't walk around on her damaged leg, even now she had a special bandage and the metal frame on it.

Whiskers didn't like the crate much and Scarlett had got quite good at fielding her when she reached in to change the litter tray or give Whiskers her food. She hated wearing the plastic collar that was supposed to stop her eating the bandage as well. But when she was quiet and purry, like she was now, Scarlett could stand there with the door open and stroke her. Anna had promised that it wouldn't be long before the frame could come off. Then they'd just have to stop Whiskers bouncing around too much while her leg was still healing.

Scarlett had a feeling that might be difficult…

"We went past the station just now on the way back from the supermarket," Scarlett told her kitten. "Tony gave me another present for you that someone dropped off! It's a toy fish that looks just like a real fish and it's got catnip in. Mum says you'd better not have it just yet though – it's going to take up too much room in your crate and catnip might make you overexcited. A couple of people asked how you were and when you'd be back at the station."

Whiskers closed her eyes and purred as Scarlett tickled under her chin.

"We popped in to say hi to Anna and Sean as well. Your treatment's all paid for, did you know that? And that means the money from the cake sale next week can be for the shelter's emergency fund, in case any other cats need help." Scarlett smiled. She was sure Whiskers had started to purr louder – she could feel the purrs, echoing through the tiny body. The kitten was all purr.

"You're our kitten now," Scarlett said. "*And* you belong to everyone at the station. And to Abbie a bit as well. You're probably the best-loved kitten there could be."

Whiskers reached one speckly ginger front paw out and pulled Scarlett's fingers closer, and Scarlett smiled.

She belonged to Whiskers too.

HOLLY WEBB

Holly Webb started out as a children's
book editor and wrote her first series for
the publisher she worked for. She has been
writing ever since, with over one hundred
and fifty books to her name. Holly lives
in Berkshire, with her husband and three
children. Holly's pet cats are always
nosying around when she is trying
to type on her laptop.

For more information
about Holly Webb visit:

www.holly-webb.com